D1317151

To my really BIG sons, Dylan, Connor,
and Chris Paratore.
I'm so proud of you and love you so much.
—CP

For Scottie, Elle, and Hope,
who inspire me to be BIG.
—CF

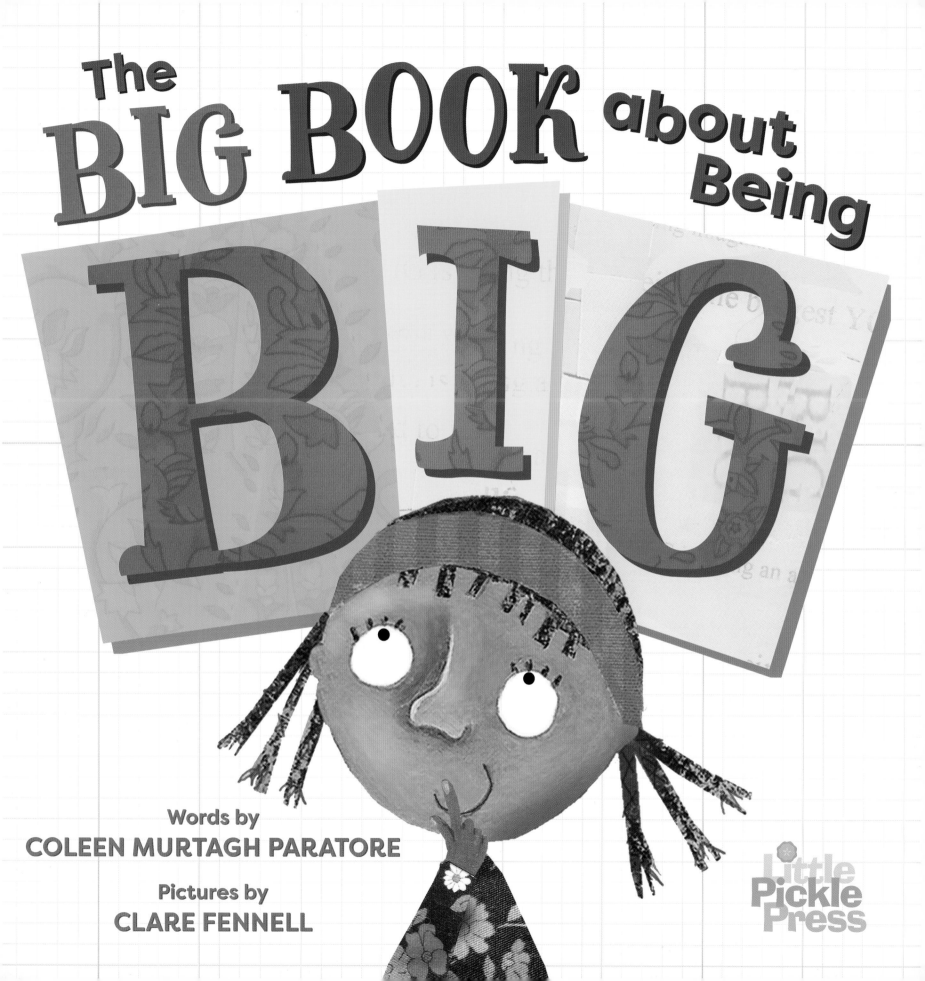

The BIG BOOK about Being BIG

Words by
COLEEN MURTAGH PARATORE

Pictures by
CLARE FENNELL

Little Pickle Press

When you were little, you wanted to be **BIG**.

BIG enough to reach that, ride this, play here, go there.

How about now? Are you **BIG** yet?

When, exactly, does **BIG** happen?

Some people say **BIG** is measured

by years, or

weight, or inches.

Others think **BIG**

is how rich you are

or where you live

or how much stuff you own.

Those people are wrong.

BIG is **BIGGER** than that. **BIG** is more.

BIG is being bright.
BIG is being healthy.
BIG is being imaginative.

BIG is being the **BIGGEST YOU** that you can be.

BIG is being kind.

BIG is being helpful.

BIG is being a valuable

member of your family, school,

and neighborhood.

BIG is being the
BIGGEST YOU
that you can be.

BIG is being an active citizen of your city, country, and world.

BIG is being a friend to the Earth.
BIG is being a friend to yourself.

BIG is being the **BIGGEST YOU** that you can be.

Each and every year, every person on the planet

gets 365 presents. You...me...everybody.

365 brand new days.

And every day, in countless ways,

we can choose to be little,

or we can choose to be **BIG**.

Brand
new day

But how will you know when you have succeeded?

How will you know when you're **BIG**?

You won't get a trophy,

a diploma, or an award.

The reward for being

BIG is invisible.

It's a pride inside,

a feeling of goodness

that makes its home

in your heart.

And here's an

IMPORTANT

thing to remember.

BIG doesn't

happen

all at once.

BIG happens little   by little.

One little thought,

one little question,

one little action,

one little change,

one little way,

one little day at a time.

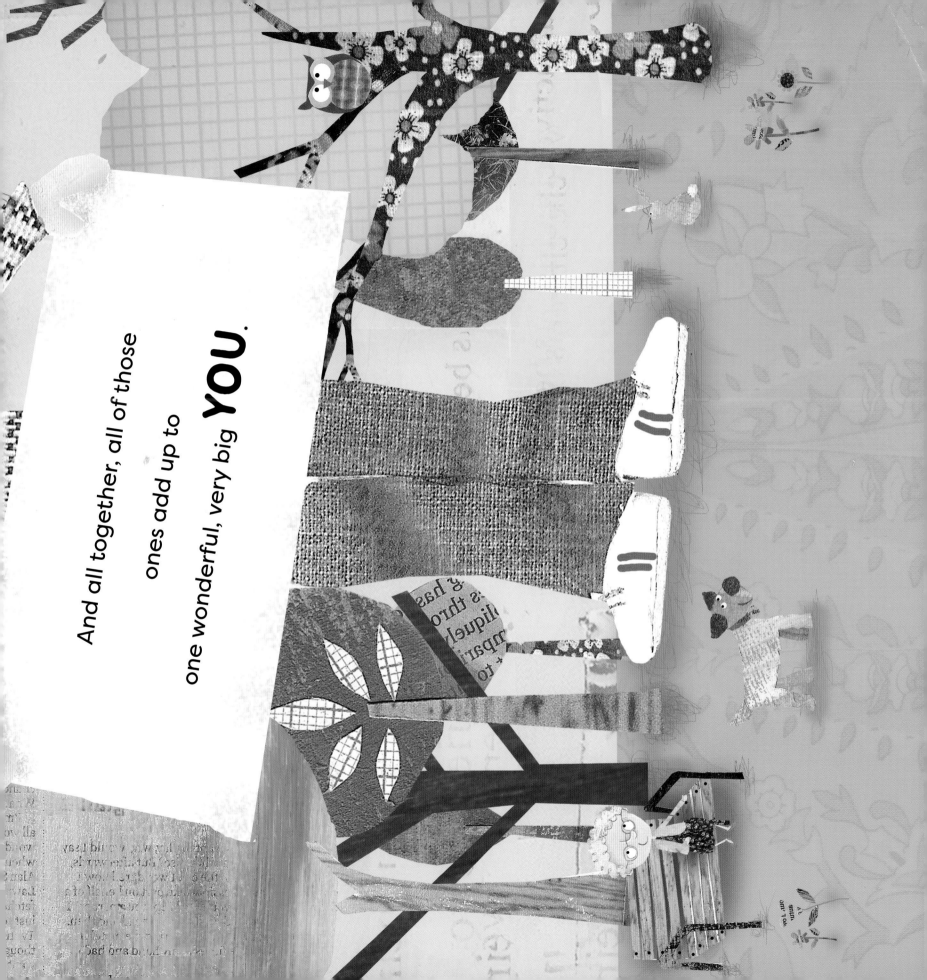

And all together, all of those
ones add up to
one wonderful, very big **YOU.**

How many little ways can you think of to be...

When will I be BIG?

Growing up can be quite the adventure. Every year, you get older and you might grow taller and bigger too. But there are times when growing up feels like it takes forever. Maybe you've been told to "wait until you're older" or "you're too little to do that." And so you just can't wait to be BIG!

But being BIG is so much more than your age or your size. Being BIG is also about the choices we make each and every day. Being BIG is about being the BIGGEST YOU that YOU can be. If you ever feel you're too small, know that you can be BIG right now!

Choose to Be Big!

Every day, in countless ways, you can choose to be little—or you can choose to be BIG. Here are some simple ways that you can choose to be BIG today!

- **Be BIG by being bright**: Read each night before you go to sleep, learn how to play a musical instrument, try out a new sport, or teach yourself some phrases in a new language. Anytime you seek to improve your knowledge and stretch your mind, you're being BIG!
- **Be BIG by making healthy choices**: Taking good care of our bodies is a great way to be BIG. You can do this by drinking water instead of soda, trying a new vegetable, and exercising every day.
- **Be BIG by being imaginative**: If you use your imagination to create something that brings joy to you and others, that's being BIG! Try writing a story, making up a dance, directing a play, or painting a picture.

- **Be BIG and be kind**: There are so many ways to be kind: sharing something with a friend, giving someone a compliment, or sending a card to someone who is going through a difficult time. Every act of kindness is a choice you've made to be BIG!

- **Be BIG by being helpful**: No matter how little you are, you can always lend a helping hand at home or at school. You can make your bed each morning, help with the dishes, or teach a friend how to do something you're really good at.

- **Be a BIG valuable member of my family, school, and neighborhood**: Can you be a good example for a younger sibling or neighbor? Have you ever been a leader in your class? Maybe you've volunteered at the food bank, pet shelter, or community center? If yes, you're being BIG!

- **Be a BIG active citizen of my city, country, and world**: You are never too young to start participating in things going on in your community. Whether you focus on things happening locally or globally, there is so much you can do to help create BIG change. Write an editorial about a good idea you have for your city and send it to your local newspaper, or write a letter to the president about an issue you feel strongly about. Even something as simple as learning about another country is a great way to be BIG!

- **Be a BIG friend to the Earth**: The Earth is our most valuable resource, and it's important to take care of it. There are so many little choices you can make to be a BIG help and keep our Earth healthy, like not wasting water, picking up litter, or planting a tree.

- **Be a BIG friend to myself**: Remember being BIG is about being the BIGGEST YOU that YOU can be! So smile at yourself when you look in the mirror, focus on the good things you do each day, or keep a diary or gratitude journal. Be BIG by embracing YOU.

These are just some of the ways you can choose to be BIG every day. But these aren't the only ways! Talk to your friends, family, and teachers to create an even bigger list of ideas. How many more little ways can you be BIG?

For more information, including lesson plans, please visit LittlePicklePress.com.

About the Author

After publishing twenty books in her first ten years as an author, **Coleen Murtagh Paratore** shares what she has learned about writing for young people with great enthusiasm. Every time she speaks about writing, she holds up her library card and says, "I am a writer because I was a reader." She credits her mother with taking her on the bus to the city library each Saturday to collect her "treasures" for the week. Coleen now lives in Troy, NY, and is the proud mother of three BIG sons, Christopher, Connor, and Dylan. In addition to writing, she gives presentations at state and national conferences and book festivals, as well as visiting schools across the country, where she enjoys meeting librarians, teachers, parents, and students.

Visit her at coleenparatore.com.

About the Illustrator

Clare Fennell left university with an illustration degree and spent fifteen years as a designer and studio manager in the UK greeting card industry before deciding to follow her lifelong dream to illustrate children's books. Clare, a mum of three kids, ousted her hubby from his beloved study set deep in the English countryside, and promptly converted it to a rather messy studio filled with children's picture books, cats, cushions, pencils, and paint. Then she set to work carving out her new career as a children's illustrator! Clare is joyfully collaging the contents of her imagination into the pages of children's books and loving every moment.

Visit her at clarefennell.com.

Little Pickle Press

Copyright © 2012, 2019 by March 4th, Inc.
Text by Coleen Murtagh Paratore
Illustrations by Clare Fennell
Cover and internal design © 2019 by Sourcebooks, Inc.
Image of world on page 15 © Freepik.com

Sourcebooks and the colophon are registered trademarks of Sourcebooks, Inc.

Published by Little Pickle Press, an imprint of Sourcebooks Jabberwocky.
P.O. Box 4410, Naperville, Illinois 60567–4410
(630) 961-3900
sourcebookskids.com

Originally published as BIG in 2012 in the United States of America
by Little Pickle Press LLC.

Library of Congress Cataloging-in-Publication Data is on file with the publisher.

Source of Production: PrintPlus Limited, Shenzhen, Guangdong Province, China
Date of Production: April 2019
Run Number: 5014502

Printed and bound in China.
PP 10 9 8 7 6 5 4 3 2 1